DREAMWORKS

CAPTAIN UNDERPANTS
THE FIRST EPIC MOVIE

WACKY WORD
WEDGIES AND
FLUSHABLE
FILL-INS

By George Beard, Harold Hutchins, and YOU!
With an assist from Howie Dewin

Scholastic Inc.

ISBN 978-1-338-19655-9

10 9 8 7 6 5 4 3 2 1   17 18 19 20 21

Designed by Erin McMahon and Marissa Asuncion

Printed in the U.S.A.   40

First printing 2017

HEY, EVERYBODY! WELCOME TO GEORGE AND HAROLD'S OFFICIAL LAFF RIOT FILL-IN NOTEBOOK!

Laffs!

Hi, I'M GEORGE BEARD.

AND I'M HAROLD HUTCHINS.

TODAY WE NEED YOUR HELP WITH OUR AMAZING ADVENTURES.

YEP! SO GRAB A FRIEND AND LET'S GET STARTED!

Action!

Thrills!

YOU WILL OBEY OUR EVERY COMMAND!

Okay, maybe not. But we do recommend you do these three things:

1. FIND A PEN OR PENCIL.
2. MAKE SURE YOU AND YOUR FRIENDS KNOW THESE PARTS OF SPEECH: NOUN, VERB, ADJECTIVE, ADVERB.
3. DON'T READ THE STORY AHEAD OF TIME. OUR ADVENTURES ARE WAY MORE FUN IF YOU DON'T KNOW WHAT'S GOING TO HAPPEN NEXT!

PRANK ARTISTS

VERB ENDING IN -ED _____

FEELING _____

PLURAL BODY PART _____

VERB _____

NUMBER _____

NUMBER _____

PLACE _____

PLURAL BODY PART _____

PLURAL BODY PART _____

ANIMALS _____

NOUN _____

FEELING _____

ADJECTIVE _____

VERB ENDING IN -ED _____

BODY PART _____

COLOR _____

VERB _____

Mr. Krupp _____ around his office. He
VERB ENDING IN -ED

was really _____.
FEELING

George and Harold covered their _____ and tried
PLURAL BODY PART

not to _____. They couldn't help but be proud of the
VERB

_____ pranks they'd pulled in their _____
NUMBER _NUMBER_

years at Jerome Horwitz Elementary School.

First, there was the Ejector Chair that sent teachers to

_____. Then there were the glue pranks that made
PLACE

basketballs stick to teachers' _____ and chairs stick to
PLURAL BODY PART

their _____. Next, there was the time they'd put
PLURAL BODY PART

_____ in the teachers' lounge and the time they'd
ANIMALS

invented the exploding _____.
NOUN

It was hard not to be _____.
FEELING

"We are _____," said Harold.
ADJECTIVE

George _____ and nodded.
VERB ENDING IN -ED

Mr. Krupp's _____ turned bright _____.
BODY PART _COLOR_

He shouted, " _____!"
VERB

BEST!
PRANK!
EVER!

This is where the magic happens. We just hang out and make comics and try to make each other laugh.

A MINI EPIC

ADJECTIVE _____

DAY OF THE WEEK _____

GRADE LEVEL _____

NUMBER _____

ADJECTIVE _____

PLURAL BODY PART _____

ADJECTIVE _____

NOUN _____

PROPER NAME _____

PROPER NAME _____

PROPER NAME _____

VERB ENDING IN -ED _____

VERB ENDING IN -ING _____

ADJECTIVE _____

PLURAL BODY PART _____

PLURAL NOUN _____

SHAPE _____

COLOR _____

PLURAL NOUN _____

ADJECTIVE _____

It was a _____ _____ in _____. George
            ADJECTIVE   *DAY OF THE WEEK*   *GRADE LEVEL*

and Harold were both _____ years old. George was wearing a
                       NUMBER

_____ tie and Harold had a bad haircut and adorably
ADJECTIVE

chubby _____.
        PLURAL BODY PART

On that _____ day, their teacher held up a _____
        ADJECTIVE   *NOUN*

that represented the solar system. She pointed to each of the planets and

began telling her students about them. " _____ is
                                      PROPER NAME

closest to the sun, _____ comes next, and then comes our planet,
               PROPER NAME

_____."
PROPER NAME

Eventually, the teacher came to the seventh planet. "This is Uranus."

George and Harold _____ around the room. All the other
               VERB ENDING IN -ED

children were _____. Their faces looked _____.
        VERB ENDING IN -ING   *ADJECTIVE*

Finally, George's and Harold's _____ met. At that moment,
             PLURAL BODY PART

they knew they would be _____ forever! Their eyes turned
             PLURAL NOUN

_____ and their faces turned _____.
     SHAPE   *COLOR*

They were the only two _____ who understood.
                    PLURAL NOUN

Uranus was _____!
           ADJECTIVE

WE APPEAL TO THE COOL DEMOGRAPHIC

PLURAL NOUN _____

FEELING _____

ADJECTIVE _____

PLURAL NOUN _____

PLURAL NOUN _____

ADJECTIVE _____

VERB _____

NOUN _____

ADJECTIVE _____

VERB _____

VERB ENDING IN -ING _____

NOUN _____

ADJECTIVE _____

PLACE _____

PLURAL NOUN _____

GREETING _____

VERB ENDING IN -ED _____

ADJECTIVE _____

FEELING _____

PLURAL NOUN _____

> C'MON, HAROLD. IF YOU WON'T DO IT FOR ME, AND YOU WON'T DO IT FOR YOU, DO IT FOR THE FUTURE GENERATIONS! SAVE TODAY'S DIAPER-WEARERS FROM A LIFE OF ETERNAL BOREDOM!

My fellow _____. Don't be _____.
PLURAL NOUN   FEELING

Things are not as _____ as you think! There are
ADJECTIVE

always _____ to pull off. We need _____
PLURAL NOUN   PLURAL NOUN

like you to carry out these stunts! So be _____ and
ADJECTIVE

_____ the battle against _____.
VERB   NOUN

If it's just too _____ to _____, then
ADJECTIVE   VERB

follow these steps to help yourself get _____.
VERB ENDING IN -ING

Stand up and grab your _____! Put on your most
NOUN

_____ clothes and head for _____. Look
ADJECTIVE   A PLACE

for your fellow _____ and shout,
PLURAL NOUN

"_____!" You will be _____ at how fast
GREETING   VERB ENDING IN -ED

you feel _____.
ADJECTIVE

It's not healthy to be _____, so find
FEELING

your _____ and get busy!
PLURAL NOUN

JEROME HORWITZ PENITENTIARY (AKA ELEMENTARY SCHOOL)

VERB ENDING IN -ING _____

PLACE _____

BODY PART _____

NOUN _____

VERB _____

BODY PART _____

VERB ENDING IN -ING _____

PLURAL NOUN _____

NOUN _____

PLURAL NOUN _____

SCHOOL SUBJECT _____

PLURAL NOUN _____

PLACE _____

PLACE _____

THIS SCHOOL SIGN IS SUPPOSED TO READ "COME SEE OUR BIG FOOTBALL GAME TODAY." SO CAN YOU EXPLAIN WHY IT NOW READS "BOY, OUR FEET SMELL BAD"??

OUR PRANKS AND PRACTICAL JOKES ARE THE LAST LINE OF DEFENSE AGAINST INJUSTICE . . .

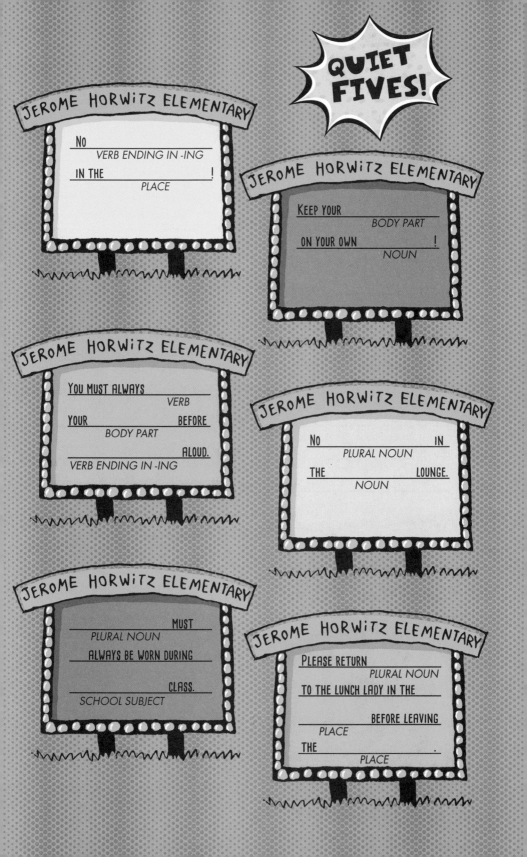

GO TO THE PRINCIPAL'S OFFICE

ADJECTIVE _____

NAME OF US PRESIDENT _____

ADJECTIVE _____

ADJECTIVE _____

ADJECTIVE _____

VERB ENDING IN -ING _____

PLURAL NOUN _____

VERB _____

PLURAL NOUN _____

COLOR _____

NOUN _____

ANIMAL _____

PLURAL BODY PART _____

VERB ENDING IN -ED _____

ADJECTIVE _____

NOUN _____

ADJECTIVE _____

ANIMAL _____

ADJECTIVE _____

FOOD _____

Principal Krupp is our _____
ADJECTIVE

leader. When he became principal,

_____ was President of the United
NAME OF US PRESIDENT

States. Mr. Krupp believes children are

_____, _____, and _____. He keeps
ADJECTIVE　　　　　*ADJECTIVE*　　　　　*ADJECTIVE*

control of the school by always _____ over
VERB ENDING IN -ING

_____ and insisting that teachers _____ under
PLURAL NOUN　　　　　　　　　　　　*VERB*

_____.
PLURAL NOUN

Mr. Krupp's favorite color is _____ because it reminds him of
COLOR

_____. His favorite lunch is _____ _____.
NOUN　　　　　　　　　　　*ANIMAL*　　*PLURAL BODY PART*

He likes them best when they have been _____ by his favorite
VERB ENDING IN -ED

lunch lady, who reminds him of _____ _____. He is
ADJECTIVE　　　*NOUN*

called Principal Krupp in public, but his friends call him the

_____ _____ and students call him _____
ADJECTIVE　　　*ANIMAL*　　　　　　　　　　　*ADJECTIVE*

_____.
FOOD

EXTRA CREDIT FEELS SO GOOD!

HINT: Time period should be words like *hour, day, year, century*, etc.

ADJECTIVE _____

NOUN _____

ADJECTIVE _____

BODY PART _____

ADJECTIVE _____

ADJECTIVE _____

ADJECTIVE _____

ADJECTIVE _____

ADJECTIVE _____

VERB ENDING IN –ING _____

VERB ENDING IN –ING _____

PLURAL NOUN _____

VERB _____

PLURAL NOUN _____

ADJECTIVE _____

ADJECTIVE _____

ADJECTIVE _____

VERB ENDING IN –ING _____

PLACE _____

NUMBER _____

TIME PERIOD _____

I WILL NOW DEMONSTRATE A PROTOTYPE WHICH I CALL THE Robotic Sock Matcher. Never waste time matching your own socks again! Patent pending.

As a well-known tattletale, I like telling people news. So it's

hard not to talk about my invention, this _____
                                                    ADJECTIVE

_____, created by my _____ _____!
       NOUN   ADJECTIVE   BODY PART

This _____ invention makes me feel very
            ADJECTIVE

_____. It's the result of _____ days and
       ADJECTIVE   ADJECTIVE

_____ nights of endless hard work.
       ADJECTIVE

But it's all worth it, because today I can announce that the

world can now celebrate the _____ _____
                                   ADJECTIVE   VERB ENDING IN -ING

and _____ Machine! No more will _____
      VERB ENDING IN -ING   PLURAL NOUN

need to _____ their own _____. My
              VERB   PLURAL NOUN

machine will do that for them, and the results will be

_____, _____, and _____.
    ADJECTIVE   ADJECTIVE   ADJECTIVE

With my invention, the world will be _____
                                           VERB ENDING IN -ING

on _____ in the next
        PLACE

_____ _____s.
    NUMBER   TIME PERIOD

SNAP!

THE HYPNO-RING MADE ME DO IT

HINT: Distance should be words like *inch*, *foot*, *mile*, etc Time period should be words like *hour*, *day*, *year*, *century*, etc.

YOUR NAME _____

NUMBER _____

TIME PERIOD _____

ADJECTIVE _____

VERB _____

BODY PART _____

ANIMAL _____

VERB _____

VERB ENDING IN –ING _____

NOUN _____

VERB _____

NOUN _____

VERB _____

NOUN _____

ADJECTIVE _____

NOUN _____

ADJECTIVE _____

ADJECTIVE _____

NUMBER _____

PLURAL NOUN _____

A PLACE _____

VERB ENDING IN –ING _____

ADJECTIVE _____

NOUN _____

NUMBER _____

ADJECTIVE _____

PLURAL NOUN _____

VERB _____

NUMBER _____

DISTANCE _____

YOUR NAME _____

We, George and Harold and _____, do solemnly
                                    YOUR NAME

confess that we have committed _____ pranks this
                                    NUMBER

_____, including but not limited to:
TIME PERIOD

The _____ Cushion that _____s into the
        ADJECTIVE   *VERB*

_____ of the person closest to it whenever a
        BODY PART

_____ _____s against it.
    ANIMAL   *VERB*

The Super-Duper _____ _____ that
                    VERB ENDING IN -ING   *NOUN*

promises to _____ your _____, but instead
                VERB   *NOUN*

_____s your _____.
    VERB   *NOUN*

The _____ Exploding _____, which looks
        ADJECTIVE   *NOUN*

_____ but is actually_____. The _____ _____
    ADJECTIVE   *ADJECTIVE*   *NUMBER*   *PLURAL NOUN*

who encountered this prank were last spotted in _____.
                                                    PLACE

The Never-Ending _____ _____
                    VERB ENDING IN -ING   *ADJECTIVE*

_____ is _____ times more _____ than a
    NOUN   *NUMBER*   *ADJECTIVE*

normal one. _____ have been known to _____ more
                PLURAL NOUN   *VERB*

than _____ _____ as a result of this prank.
    NUMBER   *DISTANCE*

We're sorry.

Signed,

George and Harold and _____
                            YOUR NAME

STOP IN THE NAME OF UNDERPANTS!

HINT: Title should be words like *Ms.*, *Mr.*, *Captain*, *Dr.*, etc. Time period should be words like *hour*, *day*, *year*, *century*, etc.

NOUN _____

ADJECTIVE _____

VERB _____

BODY PART _____

ADJECTIVE _____

VERB ENDING IN –ING _____

NOUN _____

TIME PERIOD _____

VERB ENDING IN –ING _____

PLURAL NOUN _____

NOUN _____

VERB _____

NUMBER _____

VERB _____

ADVERB _____

VERB _____

ANIMAL _____

NOUN _____

TITLE _____

PIECE OF CLOTHING _____

ADJECTIVE _____

VERB _____

VERB _____

PLACE _____

NUMBER _____

TIME PERIOD _____

Never underestimate the power of a _____. They
                                              NOUN

are very _____ when used to hypnotize people.
              ADJECTIVE

Simply _____ it in front of the person's _____
            VERB   BODY PART

and say the following:

You are getting very _____. You are _____
                              ADJECTIVE   VERB ENDING IN -ING

further and further into a dark _____. Take a very
                                          NOUN

deep breath every _____ and think about _____
                        TIME PERIOD   VERB ENDING IN -ING

_____. When I say _____, you will open your
PLURAL NOUN   NOUN

eyes and _____ _____ times. Then you will _____
              VERB   NUMBER   VERB

very _____ and _____ like a _____.
        ADVERB   VERB   ANIMAL

In the future, any time I say the word _____, you
                                                  NOUN

will become the superhero known as _____
                                                TITLE

_____. You will change into _____.
PIECE OF CLOTHING   ADJECTIVE

clothing and _____ so fast that you will _____
                  VERB   VERB

all the way to _____ in a matter of
                      PLACE

_____ _____s.
NUMBER   TIME PERIOD

WAISTBAND WARRIOR

ADJECTIVE _____

NOUN _____

ADJECTIVE _____

NOUN _____

ADJECTIVE _____

PIECE OF CLOTHING _____

VEHICLE _____

NOUN _____

PLURAL NOUN _____

VERB ENDING IN -ING _____

ADJECTIVE _____

PIECE OF CLOTHING _____

ADJECTIVE _____

PLURAL NOUN _____

PLURAL NOUN _____

PLURAL NOUN _____

VERB _____

ADVERB _____

FOOD _____

ADJECTIVE _____

VERB _____

ADJECTIVE _____

PIECE OF CLOTHING _____

Underpants . . . check. Captain . . . also check. I'm pretty sure I'm Captain Underpants!

TOP TEN MOST IMPORTANT THINGS TO REMEMBER ABOUT BEING A SUPERHERO

10. Never leave home without your _____

_____ and your _____ _____.
          ADJECTIVE

NOUN   ADJECTIVE   NOUN

9. Always wear your _____ _____.

            ADJECTIVE   PIECE OF CLOTHING

8. Always make sure your _____ is
filled with _____.   VEHICLE

       NOUN

7. When you arrive on the scene, always
confirm that the _____ are
_____.   PLURAL NOUN

VERB ENDING IN -ING

6. Never let the public see you wearing

_____ _____.
    ADJECTIVE   PIECE OF CLOTHING

5. Remember to avoid _____ _____.

         ADJECTIVE   PLURAL NOUN

4. Stay away from _____ as they
will drain your Super _____.   PLURAL NOUN

        PLURAL NOUN

3. When you _____, do it _____.

      VERB   ADVERB

2. Always eat your _____ because it
makes you _____.   FOOD

     ADJECTIVE

1. Always remember your motto: _____
the power of _____ _____!
            VERB

     ADJECTIVE   PIECE OF CLOTHING

CU

NOW I TAKE TO THE SKY LIKE AN OSTRICH!

NEVER ⭐ ✦ UNDERESTIMATE THE POWER OF UNDERPANTS!

NUMBER _____

ANIMAL _____

VERB ENDING IN -ED _____

ADVERB _____

PLURAL NOUN _____

VERB ENDING IN -ED _____

NOUN _____

NOUN _____

VERB _____

VERB ENDING IN -ED _____

ADVERB _____

NOUN _____

NOUN _____

VERB _____

NOUN _____

NOUN _____

PLACE _____

Professor Poopypants and Melvin walked into the cafeteria

like _____ _____s. They _____
    NUMBER   *ANIMAL*   *VERB ENDING IN -ED*

very _____ as they snuck up on the _____.
     ADVERB   *PLURAL NOUN*

Professor Poopypants wanted to wipe out FUN forever!

   "Ha-ha-ha!" the Professor exclaimed as he _____
                                     VERB ENDING IN -ED

his _____.
      NOUN

   "KA-BOOM!" Melvin shouted as his _____
                             NOUN

began to _____.
        VERB

   Harold and George _____ toward the
                  VERB ENDING IN -ED

cafeteria as their teachers continued to teach _____.
                                 ADVERB

   "There's a _____!" cried George as he ran
              NOUN

toward Harold.

   "It's heading straight for our _____!" Harold
                     NOUN

added. "We have to stop it or we'll never _____ again!"
                               VERB

   STREEETCH! Harold threw himself into the air and

reached for the _____.
          NOUN

   SWOOSH! George came sailing toward him.

   Together, they destroyed the _____ and made
                        NOUN

_____ safe for fun and laughter once again!
  PLACE

ZEE BRAIN OF ZEE AVERAGE CHILD

PLURAL NOUN _____

ADJECTIVE _____

VERB _____

VERB ENDING IN -ED _____

VERB _____

ADJECTIVE _____

VERB _____

VERB _____

INTERJECTION _____

ADJECTIVE _____

NOUN _____

NUMBER _____

TIME PERIOD _____

VERB ENDING IN -ING _____

PLURAL NOUN _____

PLURAL NOUN _____

NOUN _____

ADJECTIVE _____

A SCIENCE TEACHER! THE PERFECT COVER!

NEEDED: SCIENCE TEACHER

Our young _____ need a _____
               PLURAL NOUN   *ADJECTIVE*

science teacher who really understands how to _____.
                                                   VERB

Our youth are looking to be _____. Are you
                             VERB ENDING IN -ED

the teacher who can inspire them to _____ in
                                       VERB

_____ ways? Do you know how to
   ADJECTIVE

_____ and _____ to get your students
   VERB   *VERB*

to deliver their best work?

If you answered "_____, yes!" then please apply!
                    INTERJECTION

All applicants must have a _____
                         ADJECTIVE

_____ and at least _____ _____s of experience
  NOUN   *NUMBER* *TIME PERIOD*

_____ the _____. Experience with
VERB ENDING IN -ING   *PLURAL NOUN*

_____ is a plus. Benefits include _____
  PLURAL NOUN   *NOUN*

insurance and _____ retirement plan.
               ADJECTIVE

WEDGIE POWER

Time period should be words like _hour_, _day_, _year_, _century_, etc.

ADJECTIVE _____

VERB _____

VERB _____

ADJECTIVE _____

ADJECTIVE _____

ADJECTIVE _____

TIME PERIOD _____

COLOR _____

FOOD _____

VERB ENDING IN -ING _____

VERB _____

NOUN _____

VERB ENDING IN -ING _____

FAMILY MEMBER _____

ADJECTIVE _____

ADJECTIVE _____

ADJECTIVE _____

VERB _____

ANIMAL _____

VERB ENDING IN -ING _____

PLURAL NOUN _____

VERB ENDING IN -ING _____

WELL, A HERO'S WORK IS NEVER DONE!

Looking for my _____ Superhero
ADJECTIVE

I like to _____. I don't like to _____. I
VERB   VERB

am hoping to find a principal—I mean, a person—who is

_____, _____, and _____. I will
ADJECTIVE   ADJECTIVE   ADJECTIVE

make this special someone lunch every _____. I specialize
TIME PERIOD

in _____ food that smells like _____. My
COLOR   FOOD

lunches will have you _____ for more. My specialty is
VERB ENDING IN -ING

preparing tuna in ways that will make you _____.
VERB

Looking for someone to share my

_____ with . . .
NOUN

I am not good at _____. But my
VERB ENDING IN -ING

_____ says I'm _____,
FAMILY MEMBER   ADJECTIVE

_____, and _____. I like to
ADJECTIVE   ADJECTIVE

_____, especially with my _____. I am
VERB   ANIMAL

_____ as much as I can to find that person who
VERB ENDING IN -ING

would like to take _____ and go _____.
PLURAL NOUN   VERB ENDING IN -ING

Action! Thrills! Laffs! Art Class Fill-ins!

HINT: With these four fill-ins, you have to fill in the picture AND the word.

George and Harold like to snack on _____ when they create their comics.

FOOD

The sign outside Jerome Horwitz Elementary School said it was

" _____ _____ " Day at the cafeteria.

ADJECTIVE   *FOOD*

Captain Underpants shot lots of _____ at the Turbo

PLURAL NOUN

Toilet 2000, but it didn't do any good.

"Melvin, with your _____ and my

BODY PART

_____, we can wipe out laughter once and for all!"

BODY PART

HAROLD AND I HAVE A DREAM. A DREAM FOR MAKING THIS A BETTER SCHOOL FOR OUR FELLOW STUDENTS. I HEREBY DECLARE THE ART PROGRAM REINSTATED!

TREE HOUSE FREEDOM

YOUR NAME _____

BEST FRIEND'S NAME _____

ADJECTIVE _____

ANIMAL _____

FAMILY MEMBER _____

VERB ENDING IN -ING _____

NOUN _____

ADJECTIVE _____

NOUN _____

ADJECTIVE _____

NOUN _____

FOOD _____

COLOR _____

VERB ENDING IN -ING _____

FOOD _____

COLOR _____

VERB ENDING IN -ING _____

VERB _____

VERB ENDING IN -ING _____

ADVERB _____

TITLE _____

VERB ENDING IN -ING _____

NOUN _____

VERB _____

NOUN _____

WE HAVE A SUPERPOWER! IT'S THE POWER TO LAUGH NO MATTER WHAT!

THE OFFICIAL "KEEP YOURSELF LAUGHING" OATH

I, _____, do solemnly swear that I will always
    YOUR NAME

keep myself laughing. For starters, I will always call

_____ my dearest _____ _____.
BEST FRIEND'S NAME   ADJECTIVE   ANIMAL

When my _____ asks me a question, I will always
         FAMILY MEMBER

begin my response by shouting, "_____
                        VERB ENDING IN -ING

_____!" From now on, I will refer to school as My
    NOUN

Favorite _____ _____, and home will be
          ADJECTIVE   NOUN

The Best _____ _____. I will identify
          ADJECTIVE   NOUN

_____ by calling it _____ _____
    FOOD   COLOR   VERB ENDING IN -ING

and _____ will be _____ _____.
    FOOD   COLOR   VERB ENDING IN -ING

Most important, whenever I am asked to _____, I
                                  VERB

will respond without hesitation by _____
                             VERB ENDING IN -ING

_____ and shouting the words, "I am _____
    ADVERB   TITLE

_____ _____, and I am here to
  VERB ENDING IN -ING   NOUN

_____ your _____!"
    VERB   NOUN

HA HA HA

WE'RE SORRY

We really are. We're sorry that we have to go! But don't let

that stop your fun. Now that you've learned from the experts

you'll have fun wherever you go!

Just fill in the _____ with _____
                      NOUN   *ADJECTIVE*

words and you will always leave yourself and your best friend,

_____, rolling on the floor and holding your
   PROPER NAME

_____!
PLURAL BODY PART

TRA-LA-LAAAAA!